My Twelve Brothers and Me

Manufactured by Friesens Corporation in Altona, MB, Canada

08/2010   Job# 58011

Published by Second Crossing Investment Corporation

ISBN NO. 978-0-9812755-1-2

My Twelve Brothers and Me
featuring Marty Two Shoes

Written by Charles T. Sharp
Illustrated by Cara Sharp

Published by Second Crossing Investment Corporation

When I was younger I was part of the most extraordinary family, for I had twelve brothers. Each of them was exceptional. Alas, they have all disappeared in the most astonishing and sometimes mysterious ways. Creely, my youngest brother, was swept out into the ocean while surfing on a maple long john: most unusual! This story is about Marty, for he was the next to go.

After Creely's disappearance, we made a quiet and slow trip back home. Having one of 13 gone may not seem like much to notice, but we did. In a few weeks life returned to normal. Once again laughter, as well as arguments, filled our house.

Marty vanished around corners no one else could see.

Bernard painted and drew.

Ned got skinnier.

Ricochet bounced around the house.

Pete ate nuts.

Sterling studied.

Udd karate chopped most anything.

George was gentle to everyone.

Larry juggled.

Handy fixed things.

Timmy kept disappearing when chores were to be done.

And I looked after them all.

Marty was a year older than Creely and, like all my brothers, remarkable from the day of his birth. Many people are born with two left feet. It is so common that it is an everyday expression. "Oh don't mind him; he was born with two left feet." Marty, on the other hand, was born with two right feet: a very rare condition. We always had to buy two pair of shoes for him, so we could get one shoe for each right foot. After a while, we nicknamed him Marty Two Shoes.

As a baby Marty made a lot of noise.

He loved to play with the other boys,

Laughing as he brought them countless joys,

And he always lost a lot of toys.

With two right feet, walking was difficult to learn.

He tripped over ferns.

He even fell into butter churns,

But he made excellent left hand turns.

When Marty was two years old, he received a cuddly teddy bear for Christmas. It had a music box inside. When wound up, it played a beautiful tune that none of us could name. Marty loved it as only a two year old could. He called it Cubs and took it with him wherever he went.

One day, Cubs went missing. Marty was very sad. That night, in his crib, I rubbed poor Marty's back until he fell asleep. When the tears had dried upon his cheeks, I left him alone in his room for the night.

I came back an hour later to check on him. To my surprise, he was gone. I called all of my other brothers and we searched the entire house.

We checked every closet and under every bed. We peered under tables; maybe that's where he'd fled. The attic was empty; the basement was clear. How had he managed to just disappear? With tired and heavy hearts, we gave up the search.

I went back to his room to turn out the lights, and to my joyful surprise, there he was asleep in his crib. To my even greater surprise, he had his arms wrapped tightly around Cubs. What a mystery was my brother Marty Two Shoes! I didn't care; I was just happy he was safe.

I covered him with a blanket, pulled up a rocking chair and slept beside him the rest of the night. From that day on, Marty took Cubs with him wherever he went.

As Marty got older, we began to suspect what his talent might be. From time to time, one or the other of our brothers would lose something that was important or very dear to them. After a few hours, or sometimes days, Marty would disappear for a while. When he returned, he would have whatever it was they had lost.

One day we all rode the bus to the zoo. What a wonderful day it was! We saw elephants and snakes, zebras bathing in lakes, gorillas and baboons, toucans whistling tunes. We didn't want the day to end. Finally, we grew tired and hungry and rode the bus back home.

We were just about to have dinner when Bernard began to cry.

"My favourite pencil crayons," he wailed, "I must have lost them at the zoo. What will I do? I simply cannot draw without them."

"Don't worry," said Marty. "I'll get them for you. They're right around that corner up there." He pointed to an empty space in the middle of the living room.

"Wait a minute," I said taking his arm. "What corner are you talking about? I don't see anything."

"You can't see the corner?" said Marty with a surprised look on his face. "Why there are corners everywhere. They're short-cuts."

"Short-cuts to where?" I asked.

"Short-cuts to whatever is lost," he replied.

"Hmmmmm," I mused. "Well, hurry along and get Bernard's pencils. We'll talk more when you return."

Marty laughed cheerfully. He ran to the middle of the living room, made an abrupt left hand turn, and disappeared. I was amazed. Before I could say or do anything, there was a knock on the front door. I hurried to open it. There stood Marty Two Shoes with Bernard's pencil crayons in his hand. Still laughing, he walked in and handed the pencils to his brother.

"Marty, I need to know where you go and what you do when you disappear. I have to be sure you're safe," I said as I sat on the living room couch. Marty Two Shoes came and sat beside me.

"Well," he began, "there are corners everywhere. Some of them are hard to see and some are as plain as your face. I thought everyone knew about them, but I guess I was wrong. I can only go around the ones that require a left hand turn because I have two right feet. There are other corners for people that have two left feet, but I can't take those.

"Once I make the turn I'm in a big room. It's always the same. The floor has large black and white tiles that remind me of a chess board. There is nothing in the room, but at the other end there are three doors. The one on the left is blue. That's my door. The one on the right is red. That one is for people with two left feet.

"The door in the middle is the most beautiful of all. It looks like the sky on a clear night with a million stars lighting its surface. I don't know what is on the other side of that one. I want to go through it one day, but there is a big sign that says, 'ENTER AT YOUR OWN RISK,' so I leave that one alone. I always take the blue door. On the other side I'm in the place where whatever was lost was lost. Once I have the lost thing in my hands, I'm suddenly back to where I came from in the first place, or at least very close. No danger; it's as easy as eating pumpkin pie on Thanksgiving."

I thought about what Marty Two Shoes had just told me.

"It seems safe enough, and it is a very useful talent. I guess you can continue," I said.

"Great," said Marty Two Shoes jumping up from the couch. "Now what is for dinner?"

As Marty grew older, we all came to rely upon him and his unique skill. He returned to Handsome Handy a hammer he had lost. He returned to Pete Stacio some nuts at no cost. He retrieved a black belt for karate chopping Udd. He even found a juggling ball for Lefty Larry all covered in mud. As time went on, his skill became widely known.

People lined up everyday in the hopes that Marty Two Shoes would take the time to find for them whatever they had lost.

One day, Marty returned three teddy bears, two wagons, and one baseball.

On another day, he returned six pens, four rings, two hair clips and one lucky rabbit's foot.

On still another day, he returned twelve wallets, eight mittens, five shoes, three caps and one set of dentures.

Marty was getting behind at school. He had no free time to play. Yet everyday, Cubs in hand, he would face the crowd of people and try his best to find all of their lost things. Weeks passed, months passed. Marty found and returned hundreds, even thousands, of things. He seldom smiled anymore and he always looked tired. One day, after hours of finding lost things, Marty Two Shoes walked over to me and began to talk.

"Chic," he said with a wane smile on his face, "I don't think I can keep this up much longer. The more people I help, the more people ask for help. I enjoy helping them, but it is wearing me down. Now, whenever I turn a corner and go to THE ROOM, the middle door filled with stars is open just a crack. I can't make out much on the other side, but what I do see is lovely. I want to take it. Maybe there is an answer waiting for me. If only I had the courage to open the door and step through. Look." He pointed over my shoulder. "There is a corner right behind you."

He tossed me Cubs. "Here, look after Cubs for awhile. He needs a lot of love."

"Now just a minute Marty Two Shoes. You'll do no such thing. I've already lost one brother."

"Sorry, brother, but I've got to go. I think there is something good behind that door." Marty darted around me, made an abrupt left hand turn and disappeared. I looked at the space where Marty Two Shoes had been just moments before and called his name. There was no answer. I waited for an hour but still no Marty Two Shoes.

A day passed and he did not return. Then a week and then a month. My heart was sad, but finally I gave up waiting for Marty Two Shoes.

Every once in a while, either one of my brothers or I would lose something. An hour or two later, we would walk into our room and find it lying on our bed. Was it Marty or did we just forget where we had placed our belongings?

Some people said that the starry night-time door led to nowhere and that Marty Two Shoes had simply disappeared and would never be seen again.

Other people said that the starry night-time door led to a place where all the people born with two right feet went and lived happily, taking turns at finding lost things so that no one got too tired or worn out.

And that is what I believe.

Coming Soon:

GIANT GEORGE

Don't miss out on the next exciting book in the series of
My Twelve Brothers and Me.
Find out how George's incredible talent results in
his unusual disappearance.

For more information about the series My Twelve Brothers and Me
please visit our website at:

www.mytwelvebrothersandme.com

ACKNOWLEDGMENTS

A book is seldom the work of a single individual. This one is no exception. I would like to thank the following people for their help in realizing a dream:

My daughter, Cara, for her exceptional and uncanny ability to draw on paper what I see in my mind;

My two other daughters, Megan and Sylvan, who along with Cara have always been the inspiration for these stories;

Erin Williams whose unerring editorial expertise saved me from many overlooked mistakes;

Shannon (Robinson) Broza for her patient and thoughtful layout of the pages and text;

Derek Marcinyshyn whose computer wizardry goes well beyond my comprehension;

Finally, our publishers, Second Crossing Investment Corporation, for believing in all of us.

And now on to the third book; it's just around that corner up there.

Chic Sharp